Julia Caroline Ripley Dorr

Afternoon Songs

Julia Caroline Ripley Dorr

Afternoon Songs

ISBN/EAN: 9783744767538

Printed in Europe, USA, Canada, Australia, Japan

Cover: Foto ©Andreas Hilbeck / pixelio.de

More available books at **www.hansebooks.com**

AFTERNOON SONGS

AFTERNOON SONGS

BY

JULIA C. R. DORR

NEW-YORK

CHARLES SCRIBNER'S SONS

1885

Press of J. J. Little & Co.,
Nos. 10 to 20 Astor Place, New York.

TO S. M. D.

*L*ET *us go forth and gather golden-rod!*
  O love, my love, see how upon the hills,
   Where still the warm air palpitates and thrills,
And earth lies breathless in the smile of God,
Like plumes of serried hosts its tassels nod!
  All the green vales its golden glory fills;
   By lonely waysides and by mountain rills
Its yellow banners flaunt above the sod.
Perhaps the apple-blossoms were more fair;
  Perhaps, dear heart, the roses were more sweet
   June's dewy roses, with their buds half blown
Yet what care we, while tremulous and rare
  This golden sunshine falleth at our feet
   And song lives on, though summer birds have flown?

August, 1884.

Let the words stand as they were writ, dear heart!
  Although no more for thee in earthly bowers
  Shall bloom the earlier or the later flowers;—
Although to-day 'tis spring-time where thou art,
While I, with Autumn, wander far apart,—
  Yet, in the name of that long love of ours,
  Tested by years and tried by sun and showers,
Let the words stand as they were writ, dear heart!

September, 1885.

v

CONTENTS

CONTENTS.

AFTERNOON SONGS.

IT is mid-afternoon. Long, long ago
Each morning-glory sheathed the slender horn
  It blew so gayly on the hills of morn,
And fainted in the noontide's fervid glow.

Gone are the dew-drops from the rose's heart,—
  Gone with the freshness of the early hours,
  The songs that filled the air with silver showers,
The lovely dreams that were of morn a part.

Yet still in tender light the garden lies,
  The warm, sweet winds are whispering soft and low;
  Brown bees and butterflies flit to and fro;
The peace of heaven is in the o'erarching skies.

And here be four-o'clocks, just opening wide
  Their many-colored petals to the sun,
  As glad to live as if the evening dun
Were far away, and morning had not died!

SILENCE.

O GOLDEN Silence, bid our souls be still,
    And on the foolish fretting of our care
  Lay thy soft touch of healing unaware!
Once, for a half hour, even in heaven the thrill
Of the clear harpings ceased the air to fill
    With soft reverberations. Thou wert there,
    And all the shining seraphs owned thee fair,—
A white, hushed Presence on the heavenly hill.
Bring us thy peace, O Silence! Song is sweet;
  Tuneful is baby laughter, and the low
    Murmur of dying winds among the trees,
And dear the music of Love's hurrying feet;
  Yet only he who knows thee learns to know
    The secret soul of loftiest harmonies.

WHEN LESSER LOVES.

WHEN lesser loves by the relentless flow
    Of mighty currents from my arms were torn,
    And swept, unheeding, to that silent bourn
Whose mystic shades no living man may know,
By night, by day, I sang my songs; and so,
    Out of the sackcloth that my soul had worn,
    Weaving my purple, I forgot to mourn,
Pouring my grief out in melodious woe!
Now am I dumb, dear heart. My lips are mute.
    Yet if from yonder blue height thou dost lean
    Earthward, remembering love's last wordless kiss,
Know thou no trembling thrills of harp or lute,
    Dying soft wails and tender songs between,
    Were half so voiceful as this silence is!

KNOWING.

ONE summer day, to a young child I said,
   "Write to thy mother, boy." With earnest face,
   And laboring fingers all unused to trace
The mystic characters, he bent his head
(That should have danced amid the flowers instead)
   Over the blurred page for a half-hour's space;
   Then with a sigh that burdened all the place
Cried, "Mamma knows!" and out to sunshine sped.
O soul of mine, when tasks are hard and long,
   And life so crowds thee with its stress and strain
   That thou, half fainting, art too tired to pray,
Drink thou this wine of blessing and be strong!
   God knows! What though the lips be dumb with pain,
   Or the pen drops? He knows what thou wouldst say.

DARKNESS.

COME, blessed Darkness, come, and bring thy balm
  For eyes grown weary of the garish Day!
  Come with thy soft, slow steps, thy garments gray,
Thy veiling shadows, bearing in thy palm
The poppy-seeds of slumber, deep and calm!
  Come with thy patient stars, whose far-off ray
  Steals the hot fever of the soul away,
Thy stillness, sweeter than a chanted psalm!
O blessed Darkness, Day indeed is fair,
  And Light is dear when summer days are long,
And one by one the harvesters go by;
But so is rest sweet, and surcease from care,
  And folded palms, and hush of evensong,
And all the unfathomed silence of the sky!

4

GEORGE ELIOT.

Pass on, O world, and leave her to her rest!
  Brothers, be silent while the drifting snow
  Weaves its white pall above her, lying low
With empty hands crossed idly on her breast.
O sisters, let her sleep! while unrepressed
  Your pitying tears fall silently and slow,
  Washing her spotless, in their crystal flow,
Of that one stain whereof she stands confessed.
Are we so pure that we should scoff at her,
  Or mock her now, low lying in her tomb?
  God knows how sharp the thorn her roses wore,
Even what time their petals were astir
  In the warm sunshine, odorous with perfume.
  Leave her to Him who weighed the cross she bore!

SANCTIFIED.

A HOLY presence hath been here, and, lo,
   The place is sanctified! From off thy feet
   Put thou thy shoes, my soul! The air is sweet
Even yet with heavenly odors, and I know
If thou dost listen, thou wilt hear the flow
   Of most celestial music, and the beat
   Of rhythmic pinions. It is then most meet
That thou shouldst watch and wait, lest to and fro,
Should pass the heavenly messengers and thou,
   Haply, shouldst miss their coming. O my soul,
    Count this fair room a temple from whose shrine,
Led by an angel, though we know not how,
   Thy friend and lover dropped the cup of dole,
    And passed from thy love to the Love Divine!

TO-MORROW.

I.

MYSTERIOUS One, inscrutable, unknown,
  A silent Presence, with averted face
  Whose lineaments no mortal eye can trace,
And robes of trailing darkness round thee thrown,
Over the midnight hills thou comest alone!
  What thou dost bring to me from farthest space,
  What blessing or what ban, what dole, what grace,
I may not know. Thy secrets are thine own!
Yet, asking not for lightest word or sign
  To tell me what the hidden fate may be,
Without a murmur, or a quickened breath,
Unshrinkingly I place my hand in thine,
  And through the shadowy depths go forth with thee
To meet, as thou shalt lead, or life, or death!

II.

Then, if I fear not thee, thou veiléd One
  Whose face I know not, why fear I to meet
  Beyond the everlasting hills her feet
Who cometh when all Yesterdays are done?
Shall I, who have proved thee good, thy sister shun?
  O thou To-morrow, who dost feel the beat
  Of life's long, rhythmic pulses, strong and sweet,
In the far realm that hath no need of sun —
Thou who art fairer than the fair To-day
  That I have held so dear, and loved so much —
When, slow descending from the hills divine,
Thou summonest me to join thee on thy way,
  Let me not shrink nor tremble at thy touch,
Nor fear to break thy bread and drink thy wine!

A THOUGHT.

(SUGGESTED BY READING "A MIRACLE IN STONE.")

Oh, thou supreme, all-wise, eternal One,
    Thou who art Lord of lords, and King of kings,
    In whose high praise each flaming seraph sings;
Thou at whose word the morning stars begun
With song and shout their glorious course to run;
    Thou unto whom the great sea lifts its wings,
    And earth, with laden hands, rich tribute brings
From every shore that smiles beneath the sun;
    Thou who didst write thy name upon the hills
And bid the mountains speak for thee alway,
    Yet gave sweet messages to murmuring rills,
And to each flower that breathes its life away —
    Oh! dost thou smile, or frown, when man's conceit
    Seeks in this pile of stone the impress of thy feet?

A MESSAGE.

I BID thee sing the song I would have sung,—
    The high, pure strain that since my soul was born,
    Clearer and sweeter than the bells of morn,
Through all its chambers hath divinely rung!
In thee let my whole being find a tongue;
    Pluck thou the rose where I have plucked the thorn,
    Nor leave the perfect flower to fade forlorn.
Youth holds the world in fee,— and thou art young!
    O my glad singer of the tuneful voice,
Where my wing falters be thou strong to soar,
    Striking the deep, clear notes beyond my reach,
    Beyond the plummet of a woman's speech.
Sing my songs for me, and from some far shore
    My happy soul shall hear thee and rejoice!

THE PLACE.

I.

O HOLY Place, we know not where thou art!
  Though one by one our well-beloved dead
  From our close claspings to thy bliss have fled,
They send no word back to the breaking heart;
And if, perchance, their angels fly athwart
  The silent reaches of the abyss wide-spread,
  The swift white wings we see not, but instead
Only the dark void keeping us apart.
Where did he set thee, O thou Holy Place?
  Made he a new world in the heavens high hung,
    So far from this poor earth that even yet
Its first glad rays have traversed not the space
  That lies between us, nor their glory flung
    On the old home its sons can ne'er forget?

II.

But what if on some fair, auspicious night,
　　Like that on which the shepherds watched of old,
　　Down from far skies, in burning splendor rolled,
Shall stream the radiance of a star more bright
Than ever yet hath shone on mortal sight —
　　Swift shafts of light, like javelins of gold,
　　Wave after wave of glory manifold,
From zone to zenith flooding all the height?
And what if, moved by some strange inner sense,
　　Some instinct, than pure reason wiser far,
　　Some swift clairvoyance that annulleth space,
All men shall cry, with sudden joy intense,
　　" Behold, behold this new resplendent star —
　　　Our 'heaven at last revealed! — the Place! the
　　　　Place!"

III.

Then shall the heavenly host with one accord
  Veil their bright faces in obeisance meet,
  While swift they haste the Glorious One to greet.
Then shall Orion own at last his Lord,
And from his belt unloose the blazing sword,
  While pale proud Ashtaroth with footsteps fleet,
  Her jewelled crown drops humbly at his feet,
And Lyra strikes her harp's most rapturous chord.
O Earth, bid all your lonely isles rejoice!
  Break into singing, all ye silent hills;
    And ye, tumultuous seas, make quick reply!
Let the remotest desert find a voice!
  The whole creation to its centre thrills,
    For the new light of Heaven is in the sky!

GIFTS FOR THE KING.

(H. W. L., FEB. 27TH.)

WHAT good gifts can we bring to thee, O King,
 O royal poet, on this day of days?
 No golden crown, for thou art crowned with bays;
No jewelled sceptre, and no signet ring,
O'er distant realms far-flashing rays to fling;
 For well we know thy beckoning finger sways
 A mightier empire, and the world obeys.
No lute, for thou hast only need to sing;
No rare perfumes, for thy pure life makes sweet
 The air about thee, even as when the rose
Swings its bright censer down the garden-path.
Love drops its fragrant lilies at thy feet;
 Fame breathes thy name to each sweet wind
  that blows.
What can we bring to him who all things hath?

RECOGNITION.

(H. W. L.)

I.

Who was the first to bid thee glad all-hail,
  O friend and master? Who with wingéd feet
  Over the heavenly hills flew, fast and fleet,
To bring thee welcome from beyond the veil?
The mighty bards of old?—Thy Dante, pale
  With high thoughts even yet, Virgil the sweet,
  Old Homer, trumpet-tongued, and Chaucer, meet
To clasp thy stainless hand? What nightingale
Of all that sing in heaven sang first to thee?
  Through all the hallelujahs didst thou hear
    Spencer still pouring his melodious lays,
Majestic Milton's clarion, strong and free,
  Or, golden link between the far and near,
    Bryant's clear chanting of the eternal days?

II.

Nay, but not these! not these! Even though apace,
    Long rank on rank, with swift yet stately tread
    They came to meet thee—the immortal dead—
Yet Love ran faster! All the lofty place,
All the wide, luminous, enchanted space
    Glistened with Shining Ones who thither sped—
    The countless host thy song had comforted!
What light, what love illumed each radiant face!
The Rachels thou hadst sung to in the dark,
    The Davids who for Absaloms had wept,
        The fainting ones who drank thy balm and wine,
High souls that soared with thee as soars the lark,
    Children who named thee, smiling, ere they slept—
        These gave thee first the heavenly countersign!

"O EARTH! ART THOU NOT WEARY?"

O Earth! art thou not weary of thy graves?
  Dear, patient mother Earth, upon thy breast
  How are they heaped from farthest east to west!
From the dim north, where wild the storm-wind raves
O'er the cold surge that chills the shore it laves,
  To sunlit isles by softest seas caressed,
  Where roses bloom alway and song-birds nest,
How thick they lie—like flecks upon the waves!
There is no mountain-top so far and high,
  No desert so remote, no vale so deep,
    No spot by man so long untenanted,
But the pale moon, slow marching up the sky,
  Sees over some lone grave the shadows creep!
    O Earth! art thou not weary of thy dead?

ALEXANDER.

THERE was a man whom all men called The Great.
  Low lying on his death-bed, we are told,
  He bade his courtiers (when he should be cold,
Breathless, and silent in his last estate,
And they who were to bury him should wait
  Outside the palace) that no cerecloth's fold
  Or winding-sheet should round his hands be rolled:
Those helpless hands that once had ruled the state!
Thus spake he: "On the black pall let them lie,
  Empty and lorn, that all the world may see
    How of his riches there was nothing left
To Alexander when he came to die."
  Lord of two worlds, as treasureless was he
    As any beggar of his crust bereft!

TO A GODDESS.

LIFT up thy torch, O Goddess, grand and fair!
  Let its light stream across the waiting seas
  As banners float upon the yielding breeze
From the king's tent, his presence to declare.
And as his heralds haste to do their share,
  Shouting his praise and sounding his decrees,
  So let the waves in loftiest symphonies
Proclaim thy glory to the listening air!
Thou star-crowned one, the nations watch for thee,
  For thee the patient earth has waited long,—
    To thee her toiling millions stretch their hands
From the far hills and o'er the rolling sea.
  Lift up thy torch, O beautiful and strong,
  A beacon-light to earth's remotest lands.

O. W. H.

AUGUST 29, 1809.

"How SHALL I crown this child?" fair Summer cried.
  "May wasted all her violets long ago;
  No longer on the hills June's roses glow,
Flushing with tender bloom the pastures wide.
My stately lilies one by one have died;
  The clematis is but a ghost — and lo!
  In the fair meadow-lands no daisies blow;
How shall I crown this Summer child?" she sighed.
Then quickly smiled. "For him, for him," she said,
"On every hill my golden-rod shall flame,
Token of all my prescient soul foretells.
His shall be golden song and golden fame —
Long golden years with love and honor wed, —
And crowns, at last, of silver immortelles!"

A DREAM OF SONGS UNSUNG.

WHENCE it came I did not know,
How it came I could not tell,
But I heard the music flow
Like the pealing of a bell;
Up and down the wild-wood arches,
Through the sombre firs and larches,
Long I heard it rise and swell; —
Long I lay, with half-shut eyes,
Wrapped in dreams of Paradise!

Then the wondrous music poured
Yet a fuller, stronger strain,
Till my soul in rapture soared
Out of reach of toil and pain!
Then, oh then, I know not how,
Then, oh then, I know not where,
I was borne, serene and slow,

Through the boundless fields of air —
Past the sunset's golden bars,
Past long ranks of glittering stars,
To a realm where time was not,
And its secrets were forgot!

Land of shadows, who may know
Where thy golden lilies blow?
Land of shadows, on what star
In the blue depths shining far,
Or in what appointed place
In the unmeasured realms of space,
High as heaven, or deep as hell,
Thou dost lie, what tongue can tell?
Send from out thy mystic portals
With the holy chrism to-day,
One of all thy high immortals
Who shall teach me what to say!

O beloveds, all the air
Was a faint, ethereal mist
Touched with rose and amethyst,—

Glints of gold, and here and there
Purple splendors that were gone,
Like the glory of the dawn,
Ere one caught them. Soft and gray,
Lit by many a pearly ray,
Were the low skies bending dim
To the far horizon's rim;
And the landscape stretched away,
Fair, illusive, like a dream
Wherein all things do but seem!
There were mountains, but they rose
O'er the subtile vale's repose,
Light as clouds that far and high
Soar to meet the untroubled sky.
There were trees that overhead
Wide their sheltering branches spread,
Yet were empty as the shade
By the quivering vine-leaves made.
There were roses, rich with bloom,
Swinging censers of perfume
Sweet as fragrant winds of May
Blowing through spring's secret bowers;

Yet so phantom-like were they
That they seemed the ghosts of flowers.

Oh the music sweet and strange
In that land's enchanted range!
Like the pealing of the bells
When the brazen flowers are swinging
And the angelus is ringing,
Soaring, echoing, far and near,
Through the vales and up the dells,—
Softly on the enraptured ear
A melodious murmur swells!
As the rhythm of the river
Day and night goes on forever,
So that pulsing stream of song
Rolls its silver waves along.
Even silence is but sound,
Deeper, softer, more profound!

All the portals were thrown wide;
Stretching far on either side
Ran the streets, like silver mist,
By the moon's pale splendor kissed;

And adown the shadowy way,
Forth from many a still retreat,
One by one, and two by two,
Or in goodly companies;
Gliding on in long array,
Light and fleet, with silent feet,
One by one, and two by two,
Phantoms that I could not number,
Countless as the wraiths of slumber,
Passed before my wondering eyes!

Then I grew aware of one
Standing by me in the dun,
Gray half-twilight. All the place
Grew softly radiant; but his face,
Albeit unveiled, I could not see
For the awe that compassed me.
Swift I spoke, by longings swayed
Deeper than my words betrayed:
" Master," with clasped hands I prayed,
" Who are these? Are they the dead?"
" Nay, they never lived," he said;

4

"Whence art thou? How camest thou
    here?"
Low I answered, then, in fear:
"Sir, I know not; as I lay
Dreaming at the close of day,
Wondrous music, thrilling through me,
To this land of phantoms drew me,
Though I knew not how or why,
Even as instinct draws the bird
Where Spring's far-off voice is heard.
Tell me, Master, where am I?"
"Thou art in the border-land;
On the farthest, utmost strand
Of the sea that lies between
All that is and is not seen.
Thou art where the wraiths of song
Come and go, a phantom throng.
'Tis their heart's melodious beat
Fills the air with whispers sweet!
These, O child, are songs unsung —
Songs unbreathed by human tongue.
These are they that all in vain
Mightiest masters wooed amain —

Children of their heart and brain
That they could not warm to life
By their being's utmost strife.
Every bard that ever sung
Since the hoary earth was young,
Knew the song he could not sing
Was his soul's best blossoming;
Knew the thought he could not hold
Shrined his spirit's purest gold.
Look!"
     Where rose the city's gate
In majestic, sculptured state,
From a far-off battle-plain,
Through the javelins' silver rain
Bearing buckler, lance, and shield,
And their standard's glittering field,
Eager, yet with shout nor din,
Came a great host trooping in.
Burned their eyes with martial fire,
And the glow of proud desire,
Such as gods and heroes filled
When their mighty souls were thrilled
By old Homer's golden lyre!

Under dim cathedral arches
Pacing sad, pacing slow,
As to beat of funeral marches
Or to music's rhythmic flow,—
With their solemn brows uplifted,
And their hands upon their breasts,
Where the deepest shadows drifted,
One by one pale phantoms pressed.
Lost in dreams of heights supernal,
Mystic dreams of Paradise,
Or of woful depths infernal,
   Slow they passed before mine eyes.
Oh the vision's pallid splendor!
Oh the grandeur of their mien —
Kin, by birthright proud and tender,
To the matchless Florentine!

In stately solitude,
Whereon might none. intrude —
Majestic, grand and calm,
And bearing each the palm;
Dwelling, serene and fair,
In most enchanted air,

Where softest music crept
O'er harp-strings deftly swept,
And organ-thunders rolled
Like storm-winds through the wold,
They stood in strength sublime
Beyond the bounds of time,—
They who had been a part
Of Milton's mighty heart!

And where, mysterious ones,
Are Shakspeare's princely sons,
Bearing in lavish hands
The spoil of many lands?
From castles lifted far
Against the evening star,
Where royal banners float
O'er rampart, tower, and moat,
And the white moonlight sleeps
Upon the Donjon keeps;—
From fairy-haunted dells
Among the lonely fells;
From banks where wild thyme grows
And the blue violet blows;

From caverns grim, and caves
Lashed by the deep sea waves;
From darkling forest shade,
From busy haunts of trade,
From market, court, and camp,
Where folly rings her bells,
Or sorrow tolls her knells,
Or where in cloister cells
The scholar trims his lamp,—
Wearing the sword, the gown,
The motley of the clown,
The beggar's rags, the dole
Of the remorseful soul,
The wedding-robe, the ring,
The shroud's white blossoming,
O myriad-minded man,
Thus thine immortal clan
Passed down the endless ways
Of the eternal days!

Then said I to my spirit:—
"These are they who wore the crown;

Well the king's sons may inherit
All his glory and renown.
Where are they,— the songs unsung
By the humbler bards whose lyres
Through earth's lowly vales have rung,
Like the notes of woodland choirs?
They whose silver-sandalled feet
Never climbed the clouds to meet?"

Where?—the air grew full of laughter
Low and sweet; and following after
Came the softest breath of singing
As if lily bells were ringing;—
And from all the happy closes,
Crowned with daisies, crowned with
    roses,
Bearing woodland ferns for palm boughs in
    their hands,
From the dim secluded places,
Through the wide enchanted spaces,
With their song-illumined faces
Swept the shadowy minstrel bands!

Songs unsung, the high and lowly,
Songs, the holy and unholy,
In that purest air grown wholly
Clean from every spot and stain!
And I knew as endless ages
Still were turning life's full pages,
Each should find his own again —
Find the song he could not sing,
As his soul's best blossoming!

QUESTIONING A ROSE.

It was fair, it was sweet,
And it blossomed at my feet.
    " O thou peerless rose!" I said,
    " Art thou heir to roses dead,—
    Roses that their petals shed
In the winds of long ago?
Who bequeathed to thee the glow
    Of thy perfect, radiant heart?
What proud queen of fire and snow
    Lived to make thee what thou art?

" Who gave thee thy nameless grace
And the beauty of thy face,
    Touched thy lips with fragrant wine,
    Pledging thee in cups divine?

5   33

On some long-forgotten day,
When earth kept glad holiday,
     One bright rose was born, I think,
     Dewy, sweet, and soft and pink;—
Born, more blest than others are,
To be thy progenitor!

" Oh the roses that have died
     In the unremembered Junes!
Oh the roses that have sighed
     Unto long-forgotten runes!
Dost thou know their secrets dear?
Have they whispered in thine ear
     Mysteries of the rain and dew,
     And the sunshine that they knew?
Have they told thee how the breeze
Wooed them, and the amorous bees?

" Silent, art thou?   Thy repose
     Mocks me, yet I fain would know
Art thou kin to one rare rose
     Of a summer long ago?

It was sweet, it was fair;
Some one twined it in my hair,
    When my young cheek, blushing red,
    Shamed the roses, some one said.
Dust and ashes though it be,
Still its soul lives on in thee."

THE FALLOW FIELD.

THE sun comes up and the sun goes down;
The night mist shroudeth the sleeping town;
But if it be dark or if it be day,
If the tempests beat or the breezes play,
Still here on this upland slope I lie,
Looking up to the changeful sky.

Naught am I but a fallow field;
Never a crop my acres yield.
Over the wall at my right hand
Stately and green the corn-blades stand,
And I hear at my left the flying feet
Of the winds that rustle the bending wheat.

Often while yet the morn is red
I list for our master's eager tread.
He smiles at the young corn's towering height,
He knows the wheat is a goodly sight,
But he glances not at the fallow field
Whose idle acres no wealth may yield.

Sometimes the shout of the harvesters
The sleeping pulse of my being stirs,
And as one in a dream I seem to feel
The sweep and the rush of the swinging steel,
Or I catch the sound of the gay refrain
As they heap their wains with the golden grain.

Yet, O my neighbors, be not too proud,
Though on every tongue your praise is loud.
Our mother Nature is kind to me,
And I am beloved by bird and bee,
And never a child that passes by
But turns upon me a grateful eye.

Over my head the skies are blue;
I have my share of the rain and dew;
I bask like you in the summer sun
When the long bright days pass, one by one,
And calm as yours is my sweet repose
Wrapped in the warmth of the winter snows.

For little our loving mother cares
Which the corn or the daisy bears,
Which is rich with the ripening wheat,
Which with the violet's breath is sweet,
Which is red with the clover bloom,
Or which for the wild sweet-fern makes room.

Useless under the summer sky
Year after year men say I lie.
Little they know what strength of mine
I give to the trailing blackberry vine;
Little they know how the wild grape grows,
Or how my life-blood flushes the rose.

Little they think of the cups I fill
For the mosses creeping under the hill;
Little they think of the feast I spread
For the wild wee creatures that must be fed:
Squirrel and butterfly, bird and bee,
And the creeping things that no eye may see.

Lord of the harvest, thou dost know
How the summers and winters go.
Never a ship sails east or west
Laden with treasures at my behest,
Yet my being thrills to the voice of God
When I give my gold to the golden-rod.

OUT AND IN.

A SHIP went sailing out to sea,
  A gallant ship and gay,
When skies were bright as skies could be,
  One sunny morn in May.
    The light winds blew,
    The white sails flew,
   The pennants floated far;
    No stain I saw,
    Nor any flaw,
  From deck to shining spar!
And from the prow, with eager eyes,
Hope gazed afar — to Paradise.

A ship came laboring in from sea,
  One wild December night;
Ah! never ship was borne to lee
  In sadder, sorrier plight!

Rent were her sails
By furious gales,
No pennants floated far;
Twisted and torn
And all forlorn
Were shuddering mast and spar!
But from the prow Faith's steady eyes
Caught the near light of Paradise!

HER FLOWERS.

"NAY, nay," she whispered low,
"I will not have these buds of folded snow,
   Nor yet the pallid bloom
Of the chill tuberose, heavy with perfume,
   Nor lilies waxen white,
To go with her into the grave's dark night.

"But now that she is dead
Bring ye the royal roses blushing red;
   Roses that on her breast
All summer long, by these pale hands caressed,
   Have lain in happy calm,
Breathing their lives away in bloom and balm!"

42

Roses for all the joy
Of perfect hours when life had no alloy;
   When hope was glad and gay,
And young Love sang his blissful roundelay;
   And to her eager eyes
Each new day oped the gates of Paradise.

But, for that she hath wept,
And over buried hopes long vigil kept,
   Bring mystic passion-flowers,
To tell the tale of sacrificial hours
   When, lifting up her cross,
She bore it bravely on through pain and loss!

Then at her blessèd feet,
That never more shall haste on errands sweet,
   Lay fragrant mignonette
And fair sweet-peas in dainty garlands set.
   Dear humble flowers, that make
Each passer-by the gladder for their sake!

For she who lieth here
Trod not alone the high paths shining clear,
With light of star and sun
Falling undimmed her lofty place upon;
But stooped to lowliest ways,
Filling with fragrance all the passing days!

THREE LADDIES.

O SAILORS sailing north,
  Where the wild white surges roar,
And fierce winds and strong winds
  Blow down from Labrador—
Have you seen my three brave laddies,
My merry, red-cheeked laddies,
Three bold, adventurous laddies,
  On some tempestuous shore?

O sailors sailing south,
  Where the seas are calm and blue,
And light clouds, and soft clouds,
  Are floating over you,
Say, have you seen my laddies,
My three bright winsome laddies,
My brown-haired, smiling laddies,
  With hearts so leal and true?

THREE LADDIES.

O sailors sailing east,
  Ask the sea-gulls sweeping by;
O sailors sailing west,
  Ask the eagles soaring high,
If they have seen my laddies,
My careless, heedless laddies,
Three debonair young laddies,
  Beneath the wide, wide sky?

O sailors, if you find them,
  Pray send them back to me;
For them the winds go sighing
  Through every lonely tree —
For these three wandering laddies,
My tender, bright-eyed laddies,
The laughter-loving laddies,
  Whom they no longer see.

There are three men who love me,
  Three men with bearded lips;
But oh! ye gallant sailors
  Who sail the sea in ships—

In elf-land, or in cloud-land,
Or on the dreamland shore,
Can you find the little laddies
Whom I can find no more?
Three quiet, thoughtful laddies,
Three merry, winsome laddies,
Three rollicking, frolicking laddies,
On any far-off shore?

SUMMER, 1882.

R. W. E.

O SUMMER, thou fair laggard, where art thou?
In what far sunlit land of balm and bloom,
What slumbrous bowers of beauty and perfume,
Are roses crowning thine imperial brow?

Where art thou, Summer? We should see thy feet
Even now upon the mountains. All the hills
Rise up to greet thee. Nature's great heart thrills,
Faint with expectant joy. Where art thou, sweet?

And Summer answered: "Lo! I wait! I wait!
To the far North I bend my listening ear;
By day, by night, my soul keeps watch to hear
One high, clear strain that rises soon nor late!

48

" Why should I haste where light and song have fled?
   The ' Woodnotes' wake no more the Master's lyre;
   The ' haughty day ' fills no ' blue urn with fire '
When its great lover lieth cold and dead ! "

THORNLESS ROSES.

" No ROSE may bloom without a thorn ? "
  Come down the garden paths and see
How brightly in the scented air
        They bloom for you and me!

See how, like rosy clouds, they lie
  Against the perfect, stainless blue!
See how they toss their airy heads,
        And smile for me, for you!

No scanty largess, meanly doled —
  No pallid blooms, by two, by three,
But a whole crowd of pink-white wings
        Fluttering for you and me.

So fair they are I cannot choose;
  I pluck the rich spoils here and there;
I heap them on your waiting arms;
        I twine them in your hair.

There is no thorn among them all —
  No sharp sting in the heart of bliss —
No bitter in the honeyed cup —
        No burning in the kiss.

Nay, quote the proverb if you must,
  And mock the truth you will not see;
Nathless, Love's thornless roses blow
        Somewhere for you and me.

TREASURE-SHIPS.

O BEAUTIFUL, stately ships,
　Ye come from over the seas,
With every sail full spread
　To the glad, rejoicing breeze!
Ye come from the dusky East,
　Ye come from the golden West,
As birds that out of the far blue sky
　Fly each to its sheltered nest.

All spoils of the earth ye bring;
　From the isles of far Cathay,
From the fabled shores of the Orient,
　And realms more rich than they.
The prisoned light of a thousand gems,
　The gleam of the virgin gold,
Lustre of silver, and sheen of pearl,
　Shut up in the narrow hold.

Shawls from the looms of Ispahan;
  Ivory white as milk;
Shimmer of satin and rare brocade,
  And fold upon fold of silk;
Gauzes that India's maidens wear;
  Spices, and rare perfumes;
Fruits that hold in their honeyed cups
  The wealth of the summer blooms.

The blood of a thousand vines;
  The cotton's drifted snow;
The fragrant heart of the precious woods
  That deep in the tropics grow;
The strength of the giant hills;
  The might of the iron ore;
The golden corn, and the yellow wheat,
  From earth's broad threshing-floor.

Yet, O ye beautiful ships!
  There are ships that come not back,
With flying pennant and swelling sail,
  Over yon shining track!

Who can reckon their precious stores,
　　Or measure the might have been ?
Who can tell what they held for us —
　　The ships that will ne'er come in ?

CHOOSING.

MEADOW-SWEET or lily fair —
  Which shall it be?
Clematis or brier-rose,
  Blooming for me?
Spicy pink, or violet
With the dews of morning wet,
Sweet peas or mignonette —
  Which shall it be?

Flowers in the garden-beds,
  Flowers everywhere;
Blue-bells and yellow-bells
  Swinging in the air;
Purple pansies, golden pied;
Pink-white daisies, starry-eyed;
Gay nasturtiums, deeply dyed,
  Climbing everywhere!

Oh, the roses darkly red —
　See, how they burn!
Glows with all the summer heat
　Each crimson urn.
Bridal roses pure as snow,
Yellow roses all a-blow,
Sweet blush roses drooping low,
　Wheresoe'er I turn!

Life is so full, so sweet —
　How can I choose?
If I gather *this* rose,
　That I must lose?
All are not for me to wear;
I can only have my share;
Thorns are hiding here and there;
　How can I choose?

NOT MINE.

It is not mine to run
  With eager feet
Along life's crowded ways,
  My Lord to meet.

It is not mine to pour
  The oil and wine,
Or bring the purple robe
  And linen fine.

It is not mine to break
  At his dear feet
The alabaster-box
  Of ointment sweet.

It is not mine to bear
  His heavy cross,

8   57

Or suffer, for his sake,
   All pain and loss.

It is not mine to walk
   Through valleys dim,
Or climb far mountain-heights
   Alone with him.

He hath no need of me
   In grand affairs,
Where fields are lost, or crowns
   Won unawares.

Yet, Master, if I may
   Make one pale flower
Bloom brighter, for thy sake,
   Through one short hour;

If I, in harvest fields
   Where strong ones reap,
May bind one golden sheaf
   For Love to keep;

May speak one quiet word
  When all is still,
Helping some fainting heart
  To bear thy will;

Or sing one high, clear song,
  On which may soar
Some glad soul heavenward,
  I ask no more!

THE CHAMBER OF SILENCE.

One autumn day we three,
Who long had borne each other company,—
     Grief, and my Heart, and I,—
Walked out beneath a dull and leaden sky.

The fields were bare and brown:
From the still trees the dead leaves fluttered down;
     There were no birds to sing,
Or cleave the air on swift, rejoicing wing.

We sought the barren sand
Beside the moaning sea, and, hand in hand,
     Paced its slow length, and talked
Of our supremest sorrows as we walked.

Slow shaking each bowed head,
"There is no anguish like to ours," we said;

" The glancing eyes of morn
Fall on no souls more utterly forlorn."

But suddenly, across
A narrow fiord wherein wild billows toss,
  We saw before our eyes,
High hung above the tide, a temple rise —

A temple wondrous fair,
Lifting its shining turrets in the air,
  All touched with golden gleams,
Like the bright miracles we see in dreams.

Grief turned and looked at me.
" We must go thither, O my friends," said she;
  Then, saying nothing more,
With rapid, gliding step passed on before.

And we — my Heart and I —
Where Grief went, we went, following silently,
  Till in sweet solitude
Beneath the temple's vaulted roof we stood.

'Twas like a hollow pearl —
A vast white sacred chamber, where the whirl
Of passion stirred not, where
A luminous splendor trembled in the air.

"O friends, I know this place,"
Said Grief at last, "this lofty, silent space,
Where, either soon or late,
I and my kindred all shall lie in state."

"But do Griefs die?" I cried.
"Some die — not all," full calmly she replied.
"Yet all at last will lie
In this fair chamber, slumbering quietly.

"Chamber of Silence, this;
Who brings his Grief here doth not go amiss.
Mine hour hath come. We three
Will walk, O friends, no more in company."

Then was I dumb. My Heart
And I — how could we with our dear Grief part,

Who for so many a day
Had walked beside us in our lonely way?

But she, with matchless grace,
And a sweet smile upon her tear-wet face,
　　Said, " Leave me here to sleep,
Where every Grief forgets at last to weep."

What could we do but go?
We turned with slow, reluctant feet, but lo!
　　The pearly door had closed,
Shutting us in where all the Griefs reposed.

" Nay, go not back," she said;
" Retrace no steps.　Go farther on instead."
　　Then, on the other side,
On noiseless hinge another door swung wide,

Through which we onward passed
Into a chamber lowlier than the last,
　　But, oh! so sweet and calm
That the hushed air was like a holy psalm.

"Chamber of Peace" was writ
Where the low vaulted roof arched over it.
Then knew we Grief must cease
When sacred Silence leadeth unto Peace.

THREE ROSES.

" OH, shall it be a red rose, a red rose, a red rose,
    A deep-tinted red rose ? " said she.
      " In the sunny garden closes,
      How they burn, the dark-red roses,
How they lift up their glowing cups to me ! "

" Oh, shall it be a blush rose, a blush rose, a blush rose,
    A dewy, dainty blush rose ? " said she.
      " At its heart a flush so tender,
      With what veiled and softened splendor
Droopeth now its languid head towards me ! "

" Oh, shall it be a white rose, a white rose, a white rose,
    A fair and fragrant white rose ? " said she.
      " With its pale cheek tinted faintly,
      'Tis a vestal, pure and saintly,
Yet its silver lamp is shining now for me ! "

FOUR LETTERS.

(INSCRIBED TO OLIVER WENDELL HOLMES.)

[In an old almanac of the year 1809, against the date August 29, there is this record, "Son b." The sand that was thrown upon the fresh ink seventy years ago can still be seen upon the page.]

FOUR letters on a yellow page
   Writ when the century was young;
A few small grains of shining sand
    Across it lightly flung!

A child was born — child nameless yet;
   A son to love till life was o'er;
But did no strange, sweet prescience stir,
    Teaching of something more?

Thy son! — O father, hadst thou known
   What now the wide world knows of him,

How had thy pulses thrilled with joy,
How had thine eye grown dim!

Couldst thou, through all the swift, bright years,
Have looked, with glad, far-reaching gaze,
And seen him as he stands to-day,
Crowned with unfading bays —

While Love's red roses at his feet
Pour all their wealth of rare perfume,
And Truth's white lilies, pure as snow,
His lofty way illume —

How had thy heart's strong throbbings shook
The eager pen, the firm right hand,
That threw upon this record quaint
These grains of glittering sand!

O irony of Time and Fate!
That saves and loses, makes and mars,
Keeps the small dust upon the scales,
And blotteth out the stars!

Kingdoms and thrones have passed away;
  Conquerors have fallen, empires died,
And countless sons of men gone down
    Beneath War's crimson tide.

The whole wide earth has changed its face;
  Nations clasp hands across the seas;
They speak, and winds and waves repeat
    The mighty symphonies.

Mountains have bowed their haughty crests,
  And opened wide their ponderous doors;
The sea has gathered in its dead,
    Love-wept on alien shores.

Proud cities, wrapped in fire and flame,
  Have challenged all the slumbering land;
Yet neither Time nor Change has touched
    These few bright grains of sand!

VALDEMAR.

WITHIN a city quaint and old,
When reigned King Alcinor the Bold,
There dwelt a sculptor whose renown
With pride and wonder filled the town.
And yet he had not reached his prime;
The first warm glow of summer-time
Had but just touched his radiant face,
And moulded to a statelier grace
The stalwart form that trod the earth
As it had been of princely birth.
So fair, so strong, so brave was he,
With such a sense of mastery,
That Alcinor upon his throne
No kinglier gifts from life could own
Than those it brought from near and far
To the young sculptor, Valdemar!

Mayhap he was not rich — for Fame,
To lend its magic to his name,
Had outrun Fortune's swiftest pace
And conquered in the friendly race.
But a fair home was his, where bees
Hummed in the laden mulberry trees;
Where cyclamens, with rosy flush,
Brightened the lingering twilight hush,
And the gladiolus' fiery plume
Mocked the red rose's brilliant bloom;
Where violet and wind-flower hid
The acacia's golden gloom amid;
Where starry jasmines climbed, and where,
Serenely calm, divinely fair,
Like a white lily, straight and tall,
The loveliest flower among them all,
His sweet young wife, Hermione,
Sang to the child upon her knee!

Here beauteous visions haunted him,
Peopling the shadows soft and dim;
Here the old gods around him cast
The glamour of their splendors past.

Jove thundered from the awful sky;
Proud Juno trod the earth once more;
Pale Isis, veiled in mystery,
Her smile of mystic meaning wore;
Apollo joyed in youth divine,
And Bacchus wreathed the fragrant vine;
Here chaste Diana, crescent-crowned,
With virgin footsteps spurned the ground;
Here rose fair Venus from the sea,
And that sad ghost, Persephone,
Wandered, a very shade of shades,
Amid the moonlit myrtle glades.
Nor they alone. The Heavenly Child,
The Holy Mother, meek and mild,
Angels on glad wing soaring free,
Pale, praying saints on bended knee,
Martyrs with palms, and heroes brave,
Who for their guerdon won a grave,
Earth's laughing children, rosy sweet,
And the soul's phantoms, fair and fleet —
All these were with him night and day,
Charming the happy hours alway!
Oh, who so rich as Valdemar?

What ill his joyous life can mar?
With home and glorious visions blest,
Glad in the work he loveth best!

But Love's clear eyes are quick to see;
And one fair spring, Hermione,
Sitting beneath her mulberry tree
With her young children at her knee,
Saw Valdemar, from day to day,
As one whose thoughts were far away,
With folded arms and drooping head
Pace the green aisles with silent tread;
Saw him stand moodily apart
With idle hands and brooding heart,
Or gaze at his still forms of clay,
Himself as motionless as they!
"O Valdemar!" she cried, "you bear
Some burden that I do not share!
I am your wife, your own true wife;
Shut me not out from heart and life!
Why brood you thus in silent pain?"
As shifts the changing weather-vane,

So came the old smile to his face,
Saluting her with courtly grace.
" Nay, nay, Hermione, not so !.
No secret, bitter grief I know;
But, haunting all my dreams by night
And thoughts by day, one vision bright,
One nameless wonder, near me stands,
Claiming its birthright at my hands.
It hath your eyes, Hermione,
Your tender lips that smile for me;
It hath your perfect, stately grace,
The matchless beauty of your face.
But it hath more ! — for never yet
On brow of earthly mould was set
Such splendor and such light as streams
From this rare phantom of my dreams !"

Lightly she turned, and led him through
Under the jasmines wet with dew,
Into a wide, cool room, shut in
From the great city's whirl and din —
Then, smiling, touched a heap of clay.

10

" Dear idler, do thy work, I pray !
Thy radiant phantom lieth hid
The mould of centuries amid,
Waiting till thou shalt bid it rise
And live beneath the wondering skies ! "

Then rose a hot flush to his cheek ;
His stammering lips were slow to speak.
" Hermione," he said at length,
As one who gathers up his strength,
" Hermione, my wife, I go
Far from thee on a journey slow
And long and perilous ; for I know
Somewhere upon the earth there is
A finer, purer clay than this,
From which I'll mould a shape more fair
Than ever breathed in earthly air !
I go to seek it ! "

       " Ah !" she said,
With smiling lips, but tearful eyes,
Half lifted in a grieved surprise,

"How shall I then be comforted?
Not always do we find afar
The good we seek, my Valdemar!
This common, wayside clay thy hand
Hath been most potent to command.
Yet I—I will not bid thee stay.
Go, if thou must, and find thy clay!"

Then his long journeyings began,
And still his hope his steps outran.
O'er desert sands he came and went;
He crossed a mighty continent;
Plunged into forests dark and lone;
In jungles heard the panther's moan;
Climbed the far mountains' lofty heights;
Watched alien stars through weary nights;
While more than once, on trackless seas,
His white sails caught the eddying breeze.
Yet all his labor was for nought,
And never found he what he sought,
Or far or near. The finer clay
But mocked his eager search alway.

Ofttimes he came, with weary feet,
Back to the home so still and sweet
Where his fair wife, Hermione,
Dwelt with her children at her knee;
But never once his eager hand
Thrilled the mute clay with high command.
One day she spoke: " O Valdemar,
Cease from your wanderings wide and far!
Life is not long. Why waste it, then,
Chasing false fires through marsh and fen?
Mould your fair statue while you may;
High purpose sanctifies the clay."

He answered her, " My dream must wait
Fortune will aid me, soon or late!
Perhaps the clay I may not find —
But a strange tale is in the wind
Of an old man whose life has been
Shut up wild solitudes within
On Alpine mountains. He has found
What I have sought the world around.
A learnèd, godly man, he knows

How the full tide of being flows;
And he, in some mysterious way,
Makes, if he cannot find, the clay.
He will his secret share with me —
I go to him, Hermione!"

" But, Valdemar," she cried, " time flies,
And while you dream, the vision dies!
And look! Our children suffer lack;
There is no coat for Claudio's back;
Theresa's little feet, unshod,
Are torn by shards on which they trod;
And Marcius cried but yesterday
When the lads mocked him at their play.
The very house is crumbling down;
The broken hearth-stone needs repair;
The roof is open to the air —
It wakes the laughter of the town!
O Valdemar! if you must go
Up to those trackless fields of snow,
Mould first from yonder common clay
Something to keep the wolf away —

A Virgin for some humble shrine,
A soldier clad in armor fine,
Or even such toys as Andrefels
To laughing, wondering children sells."

" Now murmur not, Hermione,
But be thou patient," answered he.
" Why mind the laughter of the town ?
It cannot shake my fair renown!
A touch of hardship, now and then,
Will never harm our little men ;
And as for this old, crumbling roof,
Let rude winds put it to the proof,
And fierce heats gnaw the hearth-stone! I
Surely the Land of Promise spy.
Where the fair vision of my dreams,
Clothed in transcendent beauty, gleams!
In its white hand it holdeth up
For us, my love, a brimming cup•
Where wealth and fame and joy divine
Mingle in life's most sparkling wine.
Bid me God-speed, Hermione,
And kiss me, ere I go from thee!"

"But the rent hearth-stone, Valdemar!
Mend that before you haste afar,
That I may bake our children's bread
Till we in your high path shall tread!"

"Nay, nay, I shall return so soon!
Now, farewell! 'Tis the hour of noon,
And ere the sun sets I must be
Far on my way from home and thee!"

So on he sped, from day to day,—
Past wheat-fields yellowing in the sun,
Where scarlet-coated poppies run,
Gay soldiers ready for the fray,—
Past vineyards purpling on the hills,
Past sleeping lakes and dancing rills,
And homes like dovecotes, nestling high
Midway between the earth and sky!
Then on he passed through valleys dim
Crowded with shadows gaunt and grim,
Up towering heights whence glaciers launch
Their swift-winged ships for seaward flight,
Or where, dread messenger of fright,

Sweeps down the awful avalanche!
And still upon the mountain-side
To every man he met he cried,
" Where shall I find, oh! tell me where,
The hermit of this upper air,
Who Nature's inmost secret knows?"
And, pointing to the eternal snows,
Each man replied, with wagging head,
" Up yonder, somewhere, it is said."

At length one day, as sank the sun,
He reached a low hut, dark and dun,
And, entering unbidden, found
An old man stretched upon the ground;
A white-haired, venerable man,
Whose eyes had hardly light to scan
The face that, blanched with awful fear,
Bent down, his failing breath to hear.
" *Pax vobiscum,*" he murmured low,
" Shrive me, O brother, ere I go!"

" No priest am I," cried Valdemar.
" Alas! alas! I came from far

To learn thy secret of the clay —
Speak to me, sire, while yet you may!"
But while he wet the parchèd lips,
The dull eyes closed in death's eclipse;
And the old seer in silence lay,
Himself a thing of pallid clay,
With all his secrets closely hid
As Ramses' in the Pyramid.

Long time within that lonely place
Valdemar lived, but found no trace
In learnèd book or parchment scroll
(The ink scarce dry upon the roll)
Of aught the stars had taught to him.
Within the wide horizon's rim,
Nor earth, nor sky, nor winds at play,
Knew the lost secret of the clay.

Then sought he, after journeyings hard,
The holy monks of St. Bernard.
But they — ah, yes! — they knew him well,
A man not ruled by book and bell.
Godly, perhaps, — but much inclined

11

Some newer road to heaven to find.
And was he dead?—God rest his soul,
After this life of toil and dole!

And that was all! O Valdemar!
Fly to thy desolate home afar,
Where wasted, worn, Hermione,
With her pale children at her knee,
Beside the broken hearth-stone weeps!

He finds her, smiling as she sleeps;—
For night more tender is than day,
And softly wipes our tears away.
" Oh, wake, Hermione!" he cries,
As one whose spirit inly dies;
" Hear me confess that I have been
False to thee in my pride and sin!
God give me grace from this blest day
To do his work in common clay!"

Next morn, in humble, sweet content,
Into his studio he went,

Eager to test his willing hand,
And rule the clay with wise command.
But no fair wonder first he wrought,
No marvel of creative thought,
Not even a Virgin for a shrine,
Or soldier clad in armor fine;—
Only such toys as Andrefels
To laughing, wondering children sells!

One day he knelt him gravely down
Beside the hearth-stone, rent and brown.
"And now, my patient wife," said he,
"What can be done with this, we'll see."
With straining arm and crimsoned face
He pried the mortar from its place,
Lifted the heavy stone aside,
And left a cavern yawning wide.
Oh, wondrous tale! At set of sun
The guerdon of his search was won;
And where his broken hearth-stone lay
He found at last the perfect clay!

JUBILATE!

Jubilate! Jubilate!
Christ the Lord is risen to-day!
Hear the mighty chorus swelling
Over land and over sea!
River calls aloud to river,
Mountain peak to mountain peak —
Jubilate! Jubilate!
Christ the Lord is risen to-day!

Waken, roses, from your slumbers!
Lilies, wake,— for he is near!
Happy bells in wild-wood arches,
Ring and swing in sweet accord!

Lift your voices, O' ye maples,
Sing aloud, ye stately pines,
Jubilate! Jubilate!
Christ the Lord is risen to-day!

O thou goddess of the springtime,
Fair Ostera, thou art dead!
Never more shall priests and vestals
Weave fresh garlands for thy shrine;
But the happy voices ringing,
Over land and over sea,
Swell the mighty jubilate,—
"Christ the Lord is risen to-day!"

EASTER LILIES.

O ye dear and blessed ones who are done with sighing,
    Do the Easter Lilies blow for you to-day?
Do the shining angels, through Heaven's arches flying,
    Bear the snow-white blossoms on your breasts to lay?

For we cannot reach you, O our well-belovèd —
    Nothing can we do for you save to hold you dear;
From our close embraces ye are far removèd,
    And our empty yearnings cannot bring you near.

Once on Easter mornings glad we gave you greeting —
    Gave you fair flowers, singing, "Christ is risen to-day!"
Hands were clasped together, hearts and lips were
    meeting —
    Earth and we together sang a roundelay!

Now — yet why repine we ?— ye are done with sorrow ;
  Life and Lent are over, with their prayers and tears ;
After night of watching came the glad to-morrow,
  Came the blessed sunshine of the eternal years.

Surely in Jerusalem, where the Lord Christ reigneth,
  Ye with saints and martyrs keep this festal day—
And the holy angels, ere its glory waneth,
  Heaven's own Easter Lilies on your breasts shall lay !

"O WIND THAT BLOWS OUT OF THE WEST."

O WIND that blows out of the West,
  Thou hast swept over mountain and sea,
Dost thou bear on thy swift, glad wings
  The breath of my love to me?
Hast thou kissed her warm, sweet lips?
  Or tangled her soft brown hair?
Or fluttered the fragrant heart
  Of the rose she loves to wear?

O sun that goes down in the West,
  Hast thou seen my love to-day,
As she sits in her beautiful prime
  Under skies so far away?

Hast thou gilded a path for her feet,
  Or deepened the glow on her cheeks,
Or bent from the skies to hear
  The low, sweet words she speaks?

O stars that are bright in the West
  When the hush of the night is deep,
Do ye see my love as she lies
  Like a chaste, white flower asleep?
Does she smile as she walks with me
  In the light of a happy dream,
While the night winds rustle the leaves,
  And the light waves ripple and gleam?

O birds that fly out of the West,
  Do ye bring me a message from her,
As sweet as your love-notes are,
  When the warm spring breezes stir?
Did she whisper a word of me
  As your tremulous wings swept by,
Or utter my name, mayhap,
  In a single passionate cry?

12

O voices out of the West,
    Ye are silent every one,
And never an answer comes
    From wind, or stars, or sun!
And the blithe birds come and go
    Through the boundless fields of space,
As reckless of human prayers
    As if earth were a desert place!

A SUMMER SONG.

Roly-poly honey-bee,
  Humming in the clover,
Under you the tossing leaves,
  And the blue sky over,
Why are you so busy, pray?
  Never still a minute,
Hovering now above a flower,
  Now half-buried in it!

Jaunty robin-redbreast,
  Singing loud and cheerly,
From the pink-white apple-tree
  In the morning early,
Tell me, is your merry song
  Just for your own pleasure,
Poured from such a tiny throat,
  Without stint or measure?

Little yellow buttercup,
　　By the way-side smiling,
Lifting up your happy face,
　　With such sweet beguiling,
Why are you so gayly clad —
　　Cloth of gold your raiment?
Do the sunshine and the dew
　　Look to you for payment?

Roses in the garden beds,
　　Lilies, cool and saintly,
Darling blue-eyed violets,
　　Pansies, hooded quaintly,
Sweet-peas that, like butterflies,
　　Dance the bright skies under,
Bloom ye for your own delight,
　　Or for ours, I wonder!

THE URN.

Across the blue Atlantic waves
  She sent a little gift to me;
A golden urn — a graceful toy
  As one need care to see.

Smiling, I held it in my hand,
  Thinking her message o'er and o'er,
Nor dreamed her swift feet pressed so near
  The undiscovered shore.

Oh! had it been a funeral urn —
  The gift my darling sent to me
With loving thoughts and tender words
  Across the heaving sea —

THE URN.

A funeral urn which might have held
   Her sacred ashes, sealed in rest
Utter as that which holds in thrall
   Some pulseless marble breast!

Where drifts she now? On what far seas
   Floateth to-day her golden hair?
What stars behold her pale hands, clasped
   In ecstasy of prayer?

For ever in this thought of mine,
   Like the fair Lady of Shalott,
She drifteth, drifteth with the tide,
   But never comes to Camelot!

THE PARSON'S DAUGHTER.

"Ho! ho!" he cried, as up and down
He rode through the streets of Windham town —
"Ho! ho! for the day of peace is done,
And the day of wrath too well begun!
Bring forth the grain from your barns and mills;
Drive down the cattle from off your hills;
For Boston lieth in sore distress,
Pallid with hunger and long duress:
Her children starve, while she hears the beat
And the tramp of the red-coats in every street!"

"What, ho! What, ho!" Like a storm unspent,
Over the hill-sides he came and went;
And Parson White, from his open door
Leaning bare-headed that August day,
While the sun beat down on his temples gray,
Watched him until he could see no more.

Then straight he strode to the church, and flung
His whole soul into the peal he rung;
Pulling the bell-rope till the tower
Seemed to rock in the sudden shower—

The shower of sound the farmers heard,
Rending the air like a living word!
Then swift they gathered with right good-will
From field and anvil and shop and mill,
To hear what the parson had to say
That would not keep till the Sabbath-day.
For only the women and children knew
The tale of the horseman galloping through—
The message he bore as up and down
He rode through the streets of Windham town.

That night, as the parson sat at ease
In the porch, with his Bible on his knees
(Thanking God that at break of day
Frederic Manning would take his way,
With cattle and sheep from off the hills,
And a load of grain from the barns and mills,

To the starving city where General Gage
Waited unholy war to wage),
His little daughter beside him stood,
Hiding her face in her muslin hood.

In her arms her own pet lamb she bore,
As it struggled down to the oaken floor:
"It must go; I must give my lamb," she said,
"To the children that cry for meat and bread,"
Then lifted to his her holy eyes,
Wet with the tears of sacrifice.
"Nay, nay," he answered, "There is no need
That the hearts of babes should ache and bleed.
Run away to your bed, and to-morrow play,
You and your pet, through the livelong day."

He laid his hand on her shining hair,
And smiled as he blessed her, standing there,
With kerchief folded across her breast,
And her small brown hands together pressed,
A quaint little maiden, shy and sweet,
With her lambkin crouched at her dainty feet.

13

Away to its place the lamb she led,
Then climbed the stairs to her own white bed,
While the moon rose up, and the stars looked down
On the silent streets of Windham town.

But when the heralds of morning came,
Flushing the east with rosy flame,
With low of cattle and scurry of feet,
Driving his herd down the village street,
Young Manning heard from a low stone wall
A child's voice clearly yet softly call,
And saw in the gray dusk standing there
A little maiden with shining hair,
While crowding close to her tender side
Was a snow-white lamb to her apron tied.

" Oh, wait! " she cried, " for my lamb must go
To the children crying in want and woe.
It is all I have." And her tears fell fast
As she gave it one eager kiss — the last.
" The road will be long to its feet. I pray
Let your arms be its bed a part of the way;

And give it cool water and tender grass
Whenever a way-side brook you pass."
Then away she flew like a startled deer,
Nor waited the bleat of her lamb to hear.

Young Manning lifted his steel-blue eyes
One moment up to the morning skies;
Then, raising the lamb to his breast, he strode
Sturdily down the lengthening road.
"Now God be my helper," he cried, "and lead
Me safe with my charge to the souls in need!
Through fire and flood, through dearth and dole,
Though foes assail me and war-clouds roll,
To the city in want and woe that lies
I will bear this lamb as a sacrifice."

MARCH FOURTH.

1881–1882.

ONE year ago the plaudits of the crowd,
   The drum's long thunder and the bugle's blare,
The bell's gay clamor, pealing clear and loud,
   And rapturous music filling all the air:

One year ago, on roofs and domes and spires,
   Ten thousand banners bursting into bloom
As the proud day advanced its golden fires,
   And all the crowding centuries gave it room;

One year ago the laurel and the palm,
   The upward path, the height undimmed and far,
And in the clear, strong light, serene and calm,
   One high, pure spirit, shining like a star!

To-day — for loud acclaims, the long lament;
  For shouts of triumph, tears that fall like rain;
A world remembering, with vain anguish rent,
  Thy long, unmurmuring martyrdom of pain!

The year moves on; the seasons come and go;
  Day follows day, and pale stars rise and set;
Oh! in yon radiant heaven dost thou know
  The land that loved thee never can forget?

It doth not swerve — it keeps its onward way,
  Unfaltering still, from farthest sea to sea;
Yet, while it owns another's rightful sway,
  It patient grows and strong, remembering thee!

ROY.

Our Prince has gone to his inheritance!
   Think it not strange. What if, with slight half-smile,
Some crownèd king to leave his throne should
     chance,
   And try the rough ways of the world awhile?

Ere he had wearied of its storm and stress,
   Would he not hasten to his own again?
Why should he bear its labor and duress,
   And all the untold burden of its pain?

Or what if from the golden palace gate
   The king's fair son on some bright morn should
     stray?
Would he not send his lords of high estate
   To lead him back ere fell the close of day?

Even so our King from Heaven's high portals saw
  The fair young Prince where earth's dull shades
     advance,
And sent his messengers of love and law
  To bear him home to his inheritance !

THE PAINTER'S PRAYER.

'NEC ME PRÆTERMITTAS, DOMINE!'"

(An incident in the painting of Holman Hunt's
"Light of the World.")

"NAY," he said, "it is not done!
At to-morrow's set of sun
Come again, if you would see
What the finished thought may be."
Straight they went. The heavy door
On its hinges swung once more,
As within the studio dim
Eye and heart took heed of Him!

How the Presence filled the room,
Brightening all its dusky gloom!
Saints and martyrs turned their eyes
From the hills of Paradise;

Rapt in holy ecstasy,
Mary smiled her Son to see,
Letting all her lilies fall
At his feet — the Lord of all!

But the painter bowed his head,
Lost in wonder and in dread,
And as at a holy shrine
Knelt before the form divine.
All had passed — the pride, the power,
Of the soul's creative hour —
Exaltation's soaring flight
To the spirit's loftiest height.

Had he dared to paint the Lord?
Dared to paint the Christ, the Word!
Ah, the folly! Ah, the sin!
Ah, the shame his soul within!
Saints might turn on Him their eyes
From the hills of Paradise,
But the painter could not brook
On that pictured face to look.

Yet the form was grand and fair,
Fit to move a world to prayer;
Godlike in its strength and stress,
Human in its tenderness. ·
From it streamed the Light divine,
O'er it drooped the heavenly vine,
And beneath the bending spray
Stood the Life, the Truth, the Way!

Suddenly with eager hold,
Back he swept the curtain's fold,
Letting all the sunset glow
O'er the living canvas flow.
Surely then the wondrous eyes
Met his own in tenderest wise,
And the Lord Christ, half revealed,
Smiled upon him as he kneeled!

Trembling, throbbing, quick as thought,
Up he brush and palette caught,
And where deepest shade was thrown
Set one sign for God alone!

Years have passed — but, even yet,
Where the massive frame is set
You may find these words : " *Nec me
Prætermittas, Domine !* "

" Neither pass me by, O Lord ! "
Christ, the Life, the Light, the Word,
Low we bow before thy feet,
Thy remembrance to entreat !
In our soul's most secret place,
For no eye but thine to trace,.
Lo ! this prayer we write : " *Nec me
Prætermittas, Domine !* "

FROM EXILE.

Paris, September 3, 1879.

(A Mother speaks.)

Ah, dear God, when will it be day?
I can not sleep, I can not pray.
Tossing, I watch the silent stars
Mount up from the horizon bars:
Orion with his flaming sword,
Proud chieftain of the glorious horde;
Auriga up the lofty arch
Pursuing still his stately march —
So patient and so calm are they.
Ah, dear God! when will it be day?

— O Mary, Mother! — Hark! I hear
A cock crow through the silence clear!
The dawn's faint crimson streaks the east,
And, afar off, I catch the least

Low murmur of the city's stir
As she shakes off the dreams of her!
List! there's a sound of hurrying feet
Far down below me in the street.
Thank God! the weary night is past,
The morning comes—'tis day at last.

Wake, Rosalie! Awake! arise!
The sun is up, it gilds the skies.—
She does not stir. The young sleep sound
As dead men in their graves profound.
Ho, Rosalie! At last? Now haste!
To-day there is no time to waste.
Bring me fresh water. Braid my hair.
Hand me the glass. Once I was fair
As thou art. Now I look so old
It seems my death-knell should be tolled.

Ill? No! (I want no wine.) So pale?
Like a white ghost, so wan and frail?
Well, that's not strange. All night I lay
Waiting and watching for the day.

But — there! I'll drink it; it may make
My cheeks burn brighter for his sake
Who comes to-day. My boy! my boy!
How can I bear the unwonted joy?
I, who for eight long years have wept
While happier mothers smiling slept;
While others decked their sons first-born
For dance, or fête, or bridal morn,
Or proudly smiled to see them stand
The stateliest pillars of the land!
For he, so gallant and so gay,
As young and debonair as they,
My beautiful, brave boy, my life,
Went down in the unequal strife!
The right or wrong? Oh, what care I?
The good God judgeth up on high.

And now He gives him back to me!
I tremble so — I scarce can see.
How full the streets are! I will wait
His coming here beside this gate,

From which I watched him as he went,
Eight years ago, to banishment.
Let me sit down.—Speak, Rosalie, when
You see a band of stalwart men,
With one fair boy among them—one
With bright hair shining in the sun,
Red, smiling lips, and eager eyes,
Blue as the blue of summer skies.
My boy! my boy!——Why come they not?
O Son of God! hast Thou forgot
Thy Mother's agony? Yet she,
Was she not stronger far than we,
We common mothers? Could she know
From her far heights such pain and woe?—
Run farther down the street, and see
If they're not coming, Rosalie!

Mother of Christ! how lag the hours!—
What? just beyond the convent towers,
And coming straight this way? O heart,
Be still and strong, and bear thy part,

Thy new part, bravely. Hark! I hear
Above the city's hum the near
Slow tread of marching feet; I see —
Nay, I can *not* see, Rosalie!
Your eyes are younger. Is he there,
My Antoine, with his sunny hair?
It is like gold; it shines in the sun:
Surely you see it?—What? Not one—
Not one bright head? All old, old men,
Gray-haired, gray-bearded, gaunt? Then—then
He has not come—he is ill, or dead!
O God, that I were in thy stead,
My son! my son!—Who touches me?
—Your pardon, sir. I am not she
Fer whom you look. Go farther on
Ere yet the daylight shall be gone.—

.

" Mcther!" Who calls me " Mother"? You?
You are not he — my Antoine! You
Are a gray-bearded man, and he
Was a mere boy who went from me,

Only a boy!—I'm sorry, sir.
God bless you! Soon you will find her
For whom you seek. But I—ah, I—
Still must I call and none reply!
You—kiss me? Antoine? O my son!
Thou art mine own, my banished one!

A MOTHER-SONG.

SLEEP, baby, sleep! The Christmas stars are shining,
  Clear and bright the Christmas stars climb up the
      vaulted sky;
Low hangs the pale moon, in the west declining:
  Sleep, baby, sleep, the Christmas morn is nigh!

Hush, baby, hush! For Earth her watch is keeping;
  Watches and waits she the angels' song to hear;
Listening for the swift rush of their wings down-
      sweeping,
  Joy and Peace proclaiming through the midnight
      clear.

Dream, baby, dream! The far-off chimes are ringing;
  Tenderly and solemnly the music soars and swells;

With soft reverberation the happy bells are swinging,
  While each to each responsive the same sweet story
    tells !

Hark, baby, hark ! Hear how the choral voices,
  All jubilantly singing, take up the glad refrain,
" Unto you is born a Saviour,"—while heaven with
    earth rejoices,
  And all its lofty battlements reëcho with the strain !

Wake, baby, wake ! For, lo ! in floods of glory
  The Christmas Day advances over the hills of morn !
Wake, baby, wake ! and smile to hear the story
  How Christ, the Son of Mary, in Bethlehem was
    born !

EASTER MORNING.

Dame Margaret spake to Annie Blair,
  To Annie Blair spake she,
As from beneath her wrinkled hand
  She peered far out to sea.

"Look forth, look forth, O Annie Blair,
  For my old eyes are dim;
See you a single boat afloat
  Within the horizon's rim?"

Sweet Annie looked to east, to west,
  To north and south looked she:
There was no single boat afloat
  Upon the angry sea.

The sky was dark, the winds were high,
  The breakers lashed the shore,
And louder and still louder swelled
  The tempest's sullen roar.

" Look forth again," Dame Margaret cried:
  " Doth any boat come in ? "
And scarce she heard the answering word
  Above the furious din.

" Pray God no boat may put to sea
  In such a gale ! " she said;
" Pray God no soul may dare to-night
  The rocks of Danger Head ! "

" This is Good Friday, Annie Blair,"
  Dame Margaret cried again,
" When Mary's Son, the Merciful,
  On Calvary was slain.

" The earth did quake, the rocks were rent,
  The graves were opened wide,

And darkness like to this fell down
   When He — the Holy — died.

" Give me your hand, O Annie Blair;
   Your two knees fall upon ;
Christ send to you your lover back —
   To me, my only son ! "

All night they watched, all night they prayed,
   All night they heard the roar
Of the fierce breakers dashing high
   Upon the lonely shore.

Oh, hark ! strange footsteps on the sand,
   A voice above the din :
" Dame Margaret ! Dame Margaret !
   Is Annie Blair within ?

" High on the rocks of Danger Head
   Her lover's boat is cast,
All rudderless, all anchorless —
   Mere hull and splintered mast."

Oh, hark ! slow footsteps on the sand,
  And women wailing sore :
" Dame Margaret ! Dame Margaret !
  Your son you 'll see no more !

" God pity you ! Christ comfort you ! "
  The weeping women cried ;
But " May God pity Annie Blair ! "
  Dame Margaret replied.

" For life is long and youth is strong,
  And it must still bear on.
Leave us alone to make our moan —
  My son ! alas, my son ! "

———

The Easter morning, flushed with joy,
  Saw all the winds at rest,
And far and near the blue sea smiled
  With sunshine on its breast.

The neighbors came, the neighbors went ;
  They sought the house of prayer ;

But on the rocks of Danger Head
  The dame and Annie Blair,

With still, white faces, watched the deep
  Without a tear or moan.
" I cannot weep," said Annie Blair—
  " My heart is turned to stone."

Forth from the church the pastor came,
  And up the rocks strode he,
Baring his thin white locks to meet
  The salt breath of the sea.

" The rocks shall rend, the earth shall quake,
  The sea give up its dead,
For Christ our Lord is risen indeed—
  'Tis Easter morn," he said.

Oh, hark ! oh, hark ! A startled cry,
  A rush of hurrying feet,
The swarming of a hundred men
  Adown the village street.

" Now unto God and Christ the Lord
 Be praise and thanks alway!
The sea hath given up its dead
 This blessed Easter-day."

SEALED ORDERS.

" Oh, whither bound, my captain?
  The wind is blowing free,
And overhead the white sails spread
  As we go out to sea."

He looked to north, he looked to south,
  Or ever a word he spake;
" With orders sealed my sails I set—
  Due east my course I take."

" But to what port?" " Nay, nay," he cried,
  " This only do I know,
That I must sail due eastward
  Whatever wind may blow."

For many a day we sailéd east.
  " O captain, tell me true,
When will our good ship come to port?"
  " I cannot answer you!"

" Then, prithee, gallant captain,
  Let us but drift awhile!
The current setteth southward
  Past many a sunny isle,

" Where cocoas grow, and mangoes,
  And groves of feathery palm,
And nightingales sing all night long
  To roses breathing balm."

" Nay, tempt me not," he answered,
  " This only do I know,
That I must sail due eastward
  Whatever winds may blow!"

Then sailed we on, and sailed we east,
  Into the whirlwind's track.

Wild was the tempest overhead,
  The sea was strewn with wrack.

" Oh, turn thee, turn thee, captain,
  Thou 'rt rushing on to death!"
But back he answer shouted,
  With unabated breath:

" Turn back who will, I turn not!
  For this one thing I know,
That I must sail due eastward
  However winds may blow!"

" Oh, art thou fool or madman?
  Thy port is but a dream,
And never on the horizon's rim
  Will its fair turrets gleam."

Then smiled the captain wisely,
  And slowly answered he,
The while his keen glance widened
  Over the lonely sea:

" I carry sealéd orders.
  This only thing I know,
That I must sail due eastward
  Whatever winds may blow!"

"NO MORE THE THUNDER OF CANNON."

No MORE the thunder of cannon,
   No more the clashing of swords,
No more the rage of the contest,
   Nor the rush of contending hordes;
But, instead, the glad reunion,
   The clasping of friendly hands,
The song, for the shout of battle,
   Heard over the waiting lands.

O brothers, to-night we greet you
   With smiles, half sad, half gay —
For our thoughts are flying backward
   To the years so far away —

When with you who were part of the conflict,
  With us who remember it all,
Youth marched with his waving banner,
  And his voice like a bugle call!

We would not turn back the dial,
  Nor live over the past again;
We would not the path re-travel,
  Nor barter the "now" for the "then."
Yet, oh, for the bounding pulses,
  And the strength to do and dare,
When life was one grand endeavor,
  And work clasped hands with prayer!

But blessed are ye, O brothers,
  Who feel in your souls alway
The thrill of the stirring summons
  You heard but to obey;
Who, whether the years go swift,
  Or whether the years go slow,
Will wear in your hearts forever
  The glory of long ago!

AN ANNIVERSARY.

So long, so short,
So swift, so slow,
Are the years of man
As they come and go!

O love, it was so long ago!
   So long, so long that we were young,
And in the cloisters of our hearts
   Hope all her joy-bells rung!
So long, so long that since that hour
   Full half a lifetime hath gone by —
How ran the days ere first we met,
   Belovéd, thou and I?

We had our dreams, no doubt. The dawn
  Must still presage the rising sun,
And rose and crimson flush the east
  Ere day is well begun.
We had our dreams — fair, shadowy wraiths
  That fled when Day's full splendor kissed
Our souls' high places, and its winds
  Swept the vales clear of mist!

> *So long, so short,*
>   *So swift, so slow,*
> *Are the years of man*
>   *As they come and go!*

O love, it was but yesterday!
  Who said it was so long ago?
How many times the rose hath bloomed,
  Why should we care to know?
For it was just as sweet last June,
  As dewy fresh, as fair, as red,
As when our first glad Eden knew
  The rare perfumes it shed!

17

O love, it was but yesterday!
  If yesterday is far away,
As brightly on the hill-tops lies
  The sunshine of to-day.
Sing thou, my soul! O heart, be glad!
  O circling years, fly swift or slow!
Your ripening harvests shall not fail,
  Nor Autumn's utmost glow.

MARTHA.

YEA, Lord!—Yet some must serve.
  Not all with tranquil heart,
Even at thy dear feet,
Wrapped in devotion sweet,
  May sit apart!

Yea, Lord!— Yet some must bear
  The burden of the day,
Its labor and its heat,
While others at thy feet
  May muse and pray!

Yea, Lord!—Yet some must do
  Life's daily task-work; some
Who fain would sing, must toil
Amid earth's dust and moil,
  While lips are dumb!

131

Yea, Lord!—Yet man must earn,
  And woman bake the bread;
And some must watch and wake
Early, for others' sake,
  Who pray instead!

Yea, Lord!—Yet even thou
  Hast need of earthly care.
I bring the bread and wine
To thee, O Guest Divine!
  Be this my prayer!

THE HOUR.

WHAT is the hour of the day?
　O watchman, can you tell?
Hark! from the tower of Time
　Strikes the alarum-bell!

The strokes I cannot count.
　O watchman, can you see
On the misty dial-plate
　What hours remain for me?

I know the rosy dawn
　Faded — how long ago! —
Lost in the radiant depths
　Of morning's golden glow.

'Then all the mountain-tops
　　Stood breathless at high noon,
While earth for brief repose
　　Put off her sandal shoon.

Now faster fly the hours —
　　The afternoon is here;
O watchman in the tower,
　　Tell me, is sunset near?

Yet — why care I to know? —-
　　Beyond the sunset bars
Upon the dead day wait
　　The brightest of the stars!

THE CLOSED GATE.

I WALKED along a narrow way;
  The sun was shining everywhere;
The jocund earth was glad and gay,
  With morning freshness in the air.

The grass was green beneath my feet;
  The skies were blue and soft o'erhead;
The robin carolled clear and sweet,
  And flowers their fragrance round me shed.

How shone the great hills far away;
  How clear they rose against the blue
How fair the tranquil meadows lay,
  Where the bright river glances through!

But suddenly, as on I pressed,
 Before me frowned a closéd gate;
Filled with dismay, and sore distressed,
 I strove in vain to conquer fate!

Beyond, the hills for which I sighed —
 Beyond, the valleys still and fair —
Beyond, the meadows stretching wide,
 And all the shining fields of air!

  *   *   *   *   *

What does it mean, O Father! when
 Thy children reach some closéd gate,
Which, though they knock and knock again,
 Will not its watch and ward abate?

Still shall they batter at the walls?
 Or still, like children, cry and fret,
While the loud clamor of their calls
 Swells high in turbulent regret?

When thou hast barred the door, shall they
 Challenge thy wisdom, God of love?

Or humbly wait beside the way
  Till thou the barrier shalt remove ?

Too oft we cannot hear thee speak,
  So loud our voices and our prayers,
While to the patient and the meek
  The gate thou openest unawares !

CONTENT.

NOT asking how or why,
   Before thy will
O Father, let my heart
   Lie hushed and still!

Why should I seek to know?
   Thou art all-wise;
If thou dost bid me go,
   Let that suffice.

If thou dost bid me stay,
   Make me content
In narrow bounds to dwell
   Till life be spent.

138

If thou dost seal the lips
   That fain would speak,
Let me be still till thou
   The seal shalt break.

If thou dost make pale Pain
   Thy minister,
Then let my patient heart
   Clasp hands with her.

Or, if thou sendest Joy
   To walk with me,
My Father, let her lead
   Me nearer thee!

Teach me that Joy and Pain
   Alike are thine;
Teach me my life to leave
   In hands divine!

WONDERLAND.

THEY tell me you have been in Wonderland.
Why, so have I! No boat's keel touched the strand,
No white sails flew, no swiftly gliding car
Bore me to mystic realms, unknown and far.

And yet I, too, with these same questioning eyes,
Have seen its mountains and beheld its skies;
I, too, have been in Wonderland, and know
How through its secret vales the weird winds blow.

One morn, in Wonderland — one chill spring morn —
I saw a princess sleeping, pale and lorn,
Cold as a corse; when, lo! from out the south
A young knight rode, and kissed her sad, sweet mouth.

She smiled, she woke! Then rang from far and near
Her minstrels' voices, jubilant and clear;
While in a trice, with eager, noiseless feet,
All the young maiden grasses, fair and fleet,

Ran over hill and dale, to bring to her
Green robes with wild flowers 'broidered. All astir
Were the gay, courtier butterflies; the trees
Flung forth their fluttering banners to the breeze;

The soft airs fanned her; and, in russet dressed,
Her happy servitors around her pressed,
Bearing strange sweets, and curious flagons filled
With life's new wine, that all her pulses thrilled.

In this same Wonderland, one sweet spring day,
In a gray casket, deftly hidden away,
I found two pearls; but as I looked they grew
To living jewels, that took wing and flew.

And once a creeping worm, within my sight
Wove its own shroud and coffin, sealed and white;

Then, bursting from its cerements, soared in air,
A radiant vision, most supremely fair.

Out of the darksome mould, before my eyes
I saw a shaft of emerald arise,
Bearing a silver chalice veined with gold,
And set with gems of splendors manifold.

Once in a vast, pale, hollow pearl I stood,
When o'er the vaulted dome there swept a flood
Of lurid waves, and a dark funeral pyre
Took to its heart a globe of crimson fire.

The pageant faded. Lo! the pearl became
A liquid sapphire, touched with rosy flame;
And as I gazed, a silver crescent hung
In violet depths, a thousand stars among.

I saw a woman, marvellously fair,
Flushed with warm life, and buoyant as the air;
Next morn she was a statue, breathless, cold,
A marble goddess of transcendent mould.

I saw a folded bud, in one short hour,
Open its sweet, warm heart and be a flower.
O Wonderland! thou art so near, so far;
Near as this rose, remote as yonder star!

THE GUEST.

O THOU Guest so long delayed,
Surely, when the house was made,
In its chambers wide and free,
There was set a place for thee.
Surely, in some room was spread
For thy sake a snowy bed,
Decked with linen white and fine,
Meet, O Guest, for use of thine.

Yet thou hast not kept the tryst.
Other guests our lips have kissed:
Other guests have tarried long,
Wooed by sunshine and by song;
For the year was bright with May,
All the birds kept holiday,
All the skies were clear and blue,
When this house of ours was new.

Youth came in with us to dwell,
Crowned with rose and asphodel,
Lingered long, and even yet
Cannot quite his haunts forget.
Love hath sat beside our board,
Brought us treasures from his hoard,
Brimmed our cups with fragrant wine,
Vintage of the hills divine.

Down our garden path has strayed
Young Romance, in light arrayed;
Joy hath flung her garlands wide ·
Faith sung low at eventide;
Care hath flitted in and out;
Sorrow strewn her weeds about;
Hope held up her torch on high
When clouds darkened all the sky.

Pain, with pallid lips and thin,
Oft hath slept our house within;
Life hath called us, loud and long,
With a voice as trumpet strong.

Sometimes we have thought, O Guest,
Thou wert coming with the rest,
Watched to see thy shadow fall
On the inner chamber wall.

For we know that, soon or late,
Thou wilt enter at the gate,
Cross the threshold, pass the door,
Glide at will from floor to floor.
When thou comest, by this sign
We shall know thee, Guest divine:
Though alone thy coming be,
Some one must go forth with thee!

FORESHADOWINGS.

WIND of the winter night,
  Under the starry skies
Somewhere my lady bright,
    Slumbering, lies.
Wrapped in calm maiden dreams,
Where the pale moonlight streams,
    Softly she sleeps.

I do not know her face,
  Pure as the lonely star
That in yon darkling space
    Shineth afar;
Never with soft command
Touched I her willing hand,
    Kissed I her lips.

147

I have not heard her voice,
  I do not know her name;
Yet doth my heart rejoice,
  Owning her claim;
Yet am I true to her;
All that is due to her
  Sacred I keep.

Never a thought of me
  Troubles her soft repose;
Courant of mine may be
  Lily nor rose.
They may not bear to her
This heart's fond prayer to her,
  Yet — she is mine.

Wind of the winter night,
  Over the fields of snow,
Over the hills so white,
  Tenderly blow!
Somewhere red roses bloom;
Into her warm, hushed room,
  Bear thou their breath.

Whisper — Nay, nay, thou sprite,
　Breathe thou no tender word;
Wind of the winter night,
　　Die thou unheard.
True love shall yet prevail,
Telling its own sweet tale:
　　Till then I wait.

AN OLD-FASHIONED GARDEN.

An old-fashioned garden? Yes, my dear,
No doubt it is. I was thinking here
Only to-day, as I sat in the sun,
How fair was the scene I looked upon;
Yet wondered still, with a vague surprise,
How it might look to other eyes.

'Tis a wide old garden. Not a bed
Cut here and there in the turf; instead,
The broad straight paths run east and west,
Down which two horsemen could ride abreast,
And north and south with an equal state,
From the gray stone wall to the low white gate.

And, where they cross on the middle line,
Virgin's-bower and wild woodbine
Clamber and climb at their own sweet will
Over the latticed arbor still;
Though, since they were planted, years have flown,
And many a time have the roses blown.

To the right the hill runs down to the river,
Where the willows droop and the aspens shiver,
And under the shade of the hemlock-trees
The low ferns nod to the passing breeze;
There wild flowers blossom, and mosses creep
With a tangle of vines o'er the wooded steep.

So quiet it is, so cool and still,
In the green retreat of the shady hill!
And you scarce can tell, as you look within,
Where the garden ends and the woods begin.
But here, where we stand, what a blaze of light,
What a wealth of color, makes glad the sight!

Red roses burn in the morning glow;
White roses proffer their cups of snow;
In scarlet and crimson and cloth-of-gold
The zinnias flaunt, and the marigold;
And stately and tall the lilies stand,
Like vestal virgins, on either hand.

Here gay sweet-peas, like butterflies,
Flutter and dance under summer skies;
Blue violets here in the shade are set,
With a border of fragrant mignonette;
And here are pansies and columbine,
And the burning stars of the cypress-vine.

Stately hollyhocks, row on row,
Golden sunflowers, all aglow,
Scarlet poppies, and larkspurs blue,
Asters of every shade and hue;
And over the wall, like a trail of fire,
The red nasturtium climbs high and higher.

My lady's-slippers are fair to see,
And her pinks are as sweet as sweet can be,
With gillyflowers and mourning-brides,
And many another flower besides.
Do you see that rose without a thorn?
It was planted the year my Hal was born.

And he is a man now. Yes, my dear,
An old-fashioned garden! But, sitting here,
I think how often lover and maid
Down these long flowery paths have strayed,
And how little feet have over them run
That will stir no more in shade or sun.

As one who reads from an open book,
On these fair luminous scrolls I look;
And all the story of life is there,—
Its loves and losses, hope and despair.
An old-fashioned garden — but to my eyes
Fair as the hills of Paradise.

20

DISCONTENT.

I.

(The Brier Rose speaks.)

I CLING to the garden wall
  Outside, where the grasses grow;
Where the tall weeds flaunt in the sun,
  And the yellow mulleins blow.
The dock and the thistle crowd
  Close to my shrinking feet,
And the gypsy yarrow shares
  My cup and the food I eat.

The rude winds toss my hair,
  The wild rains beat me down,
The way-side dust lies white
  And thick on my leafy crown.

154

I cannot keep my robes
　From wanton fingers free,
And the veriest beggar dares
　To stop and gaze at me.

Sometimes I climb and climb
　To the top of the garden wall,
And I see her where she stands,
　Stately and fair and tall —
My sister, the red, red Rose,
　My sister, the royal one,
The fairest flower that blows
　Under the summer sun!

What wonder that she is fair?
　What wonder that she is sweet?
The treasures of earth and air
　Lie at her dainty feet;
The choicest fare is hers,
　Her cup is brimmed with wine;
Rich are her emerald robes,
　And her bed is soft and fine.

She need not lift her head
   Even to sip the dew;
No rude touch makes her shrink
   The whole long summer through.
Her servants do her will;
   They come at her beck and call.
Oh, rare is life in my lady's bowers
   Inside of the garden wall!

II.

(The Garden Rose speaks.)

The garden path runs east,
   And the garden path runs west;
There's a tree by the garden gate,
   And a little bird in a nest.
It sings and sings and sings!
   Does the bird, I wonder, know
How, over the garden wall,
   The bright days come and go?

The garden path runs north,
  And the garden path runs south;
The brown bee hums in the sun,
  And kisses the lily's mouth;
But it flies away, away,
  To the birch-tree, dark and tall.
What do you find, O brown bee,
  Over the garden wall?

With ruff and farthingale,
  Under the gardener's eye,
In trimmest guise I stand —
  Oh, who so fine as I?
But even the light wind knows
  That it may not play with me,
Nor touch my beautiful lips
  With a wild caress and free.

Oh, straight is the garden path,
  And smooth is the garden bed,
Where never an idle weed
  Dares lift its careless head.

But I know outside the wall
 They gather, a merry throng;
They dance and flutter and sing,
 And I listen all day long.

The Brier Rose swings outside;
 Sometimes she climbs so high
I can see her sweet pink face
 Against the blue of the sky.
What wonder that she is fair,
 Whom no strait bonds enthrall?
Oh, rare is life to the Brier Rose,
 Outside of the garden wall!

THE DOVES AT MENDON.

"Coo! coo! coo!" says Arné,
Calling the doves at Mendon!

Under the vine-clad porch she stands,
A gentle maiden with willing hands,
Dropping the grains of yellow corn.
Low and soft, like a mellow horn,
While the sunshine over her falls,
Over and over she calls and calls
    "Coo! coo! coo!" to the doves —
    The happy doves at Mendon.

    "Coo! coo! coo!" says Arné,
    Calling the doves at Mendon!

With a rush and a whir of shining wings,
They hear and obey — the dainty things!
Dun and purple and snowy white,
Clouded gray, like the soft twilight,
Straight as an arrow shot from a bow,
Wheeling and circling high and low,
    Down they fly from the slanting roof
    Of the old red barn at Mendon.

    "Coo! coo! coo!" says Arné,
    Calling the doves at Mendon!

Baby Alice with wide blue eyes
Watches them ever with new surprise,
While she and Wag on the mat together
Joy in the soft midsummer weather.
Hither and thither she sees them fly,
Gray and white on the azure sky,
    Light and shadow against the green
    Of the maple grove at Mendon.

    "Coo! coo! coo!" says Arné,
    Calling the doves at Mendon!

Down they flutter with timid grace,
Lured by the voice and the tender face,
Till the evening air is all astir
With the happy strife and the eager whir.
One by one, and two by two,
And then a rush through the ether blue;
    While Arné scatters the yellow corn
    For the gentle doves at Mendon.

    " Coo! coo! coo!" says Arné,
    Calling the doves at Mendon!

They hop on the porch where the baby sits,
They come and go, as a shadow flits,
Now here, now there, while in and out
They crowd and jostle each other about;
Till one, grown bolder than all the rest,—
A snow-white dove with an arching breast,—
    Softly lights on her outstretched hand
    Under the vines at Mendon.

    " Coo! coo! coo!" says Arné,
    Calling the doves at Mendon!

21

A sound, a motion, a flash of wings,—
They are gone — like a dream of heavenly things
The doves have flown and the porch is still,
And the shadows gather on vale and hill.
Then sinks the sun, and the mountain breeze
Stirs in the tremulous maple trees;
> While Love and Peace, as the night comes
> down,
> Brood over quiet Mendon!

A LATE ROSE.

I SENT a little maiden
  To pluck for me a rose,
The sweetest and the fairest
  That in the garden grows,—
A blush-rose, proud and tender,
Upon its stem so slender,
Swaying in dreamy splendor
  Where yellow sunshine glows.

Back came the little maiden
  With drooping, downcast head,
And slow, reluctant footsteps,
  And this to me she said:
" I find no sweet blush-roses
In all the garden-closes:
There are no summer roses;
  It must be they are dead ! "

Then bent I to the maiden
  And touched her shining hair,—
Dear heart! in all the garden
  Was nothing half so fair!
" Nay!" said I, "let the roses
Die in the garden-closes
Whenever fate disposes,
  If I *this* rose may wear!"

PERIWINKLE.

TINKLE, tinkle,
Periwinkle!
Soft and clear,
Far or near,
Still the mellow notes I hear!
Up and down the sunny hills,
Here you go, there you go,
Where the happy mountain rills
Tinkle soft, tinkle low;
Where the willows, all a-quiver,
Dip their long wands in the river,
And the hemlock shadows fall
By the gray rocks, cool and tall—
In and out,
And round about,
Here you go,
There you go!

PERIWINKLE.

Tinkle, tinkle,
Periwinkle!
Here and there,
Everywhere,
Floats the music on the air!
Through the pastures wide and free,
Here you go, there you go,
Making friends with bird and bee,
Flying high, flying low;
In and out, where lilies blowing
Nod above wild grasses growing,
Where the sweet-fern and the brake
All around rich odors make,
Where the mosses cling and creep
To the rocks, and up the steep —
In and out
You wind about,
Here and there,
Everywhere!

Tinkle, tinkle,
Periwinkle!

Day is done,
And the sun
Now its royal couch hath won!
Homeward through the winding lane,
Here you go, there you go,
While the bell in sweet refrain
Tinkles clear, tinkles low,—
Tinkles softly through the gloaming,
"Drop the bars — I'm tired of roaming
Here and there, everywhere
Through the pastures wide and fair.
Home is best,
Home and rest!"
Through the bars goes Periwinkle,
While the bell goes tinkle, tinkle,
Low and clear,
Saying softly, "Night is here!"

AFTERNOON.

O PERFECT day,
I bid thee stay!
Too fast thy glad hours slip away;
The morn, the noon,
Have fled too soon,—
Delay, O golden afternoon!

O peerless Sun,
Thou radiant one
Whose dazzling course is half-way run,
Stay, stay thy flight
Down yon blue height,
Nor haste thee to the arms of night!

The west wind blows
O'er beds of rose,
But does not stir my deep repose.

In dreamful guise
I close mine eyes,
Borne on its wings to Paradise.

Beneath this tree
Half consciously
I share the life of all things free,
Hearing the beat
Of rhythmic feet,
As the grasses run my hand to meet.

The wild bee's hum,
The lone bird's drum,
O'er the wide pastures faintly come;
And soft and clear
Falls on my ear
The cow-bell's tinkle, far and near!

Before my eyes
Three blue peaks rise,
Piercing the bright autumnal skies;

Silent and grand,
On either hand,
Far mountain heights majestic stand.

By wreaths of mist
The vales are kissed,—
Fair, floating clouds of amethyst,
That follow on,
Through shade and sun,
Where'er the river's course may run.

Here, looking down
On rooftrees brown,
I catch fair glimpses of the town.
There, far away,
The shadows play
On crags and boulders, huge and gray.

All whispering low,
The breezes go,—
The wandering birds flit to and fro;

Winged motes float by
Me as I lie,
And yellow leaves drop silently.

The morn, the noon,
Have fled too soon,—
Delay, O golden afternoon,
While with rapt eyes
My spirit flies
From yon blue peaks to Paradise!

THE LADY OF THE PROW.

BERMUDA, MAY, 1883.

THE salt tides ebb, the salt tides flow,
From the near isles the soft airs blow;
From leagues remote, with roar and din,
Over the reefs the waves rush in;
The wild white breakers foam and fret,
Day follows day, stars rise and set;
Yet, grandly poised, as calm and fair
As some proud spirit of the air,
Unmoved she lifts her radiant brow,—
She, the White Lady of the Prow!

The winds blow east, the winds blow west,
From woodlands low to the eagle's nest;
The winds blow north, the winds blow south,
To steal the sweets from the lily's mouth!

We come and go; we spread our sails
Like sea-gulls to the favoring gales;
Or, soft and slow, our oars we dip
Under the lee of the stranded ship.
Yet little recks she when or how,
The grand White Lady of the Prow.

We laugh, we love, we smile, we sigh,
But never she heeds as we glide by,—
Never she cares for our idle ways,
Nor turns from the brink of the world her gaze!
What does she see when her steadfast eyes
Peer into the sunset mysteries,
And all the secrets of time and space
Seem unfolded before her face?
What does she hear when, pale and calm,
She lists for the great sea's evening psalm?

Speak, Lady, speak! Thy sealèd lip,
Thou fair white spirit of the ship,
Could tell such tales of high emprise,
Of valorous deeds and counsels wise!

What prince shall rouse thee from thy trance,
And meet thy first revealing glance,
Or what Pygmalion from her sleep
Bid Galatea wake and weep?
The wave's wild passion stirs thee not,—
Oh, is thy life's long love forgot?

How canst thou bear this trancèd calm
By sunlit isles of bloom and balm,—
Thou who hast sailed the utmost seas,
Empress alike of wave and breeze;
Thou who hast swept from pole to pole,
Where the great surges swell and roll;
Breasted the billows white with wrath,
Rode in the tempest's fiery path,
And proudly borne to waiting hands
The glorious spoil of farthest lands?

How canst thou bear this silence, deep
And tranquil as an infant's sleep,—
Thou who hast heard above thy head
The white sails sing with wings outspread;

Thou whose strong soul has thrilled to feel
The swift rush of the ploughing keel,
The dash of waves, and the wild uproar
Of ocean lashed from shore to shore?
How canst thou bear this changeless rest,
Thou who hast made the world thy quest?

O Lady of the stranded ship,
Once more our lingering oars we dip
In the clear blue that round thee lies,
Fanned by the airs of Paradise!
Farewell! farewell! But oft when day
On our far hill-tops dies away,
And night's cool winds the pine-trees bow,
Our eyes will see thee, even as now,
Waiting — a spirit pale and calm —
To hear the great sea's evening psalm!

GRANT.

AUGUST 8, 1885.

GOD sends his angels where he will,
  From world to world, from star to star;
They do his bidding as they fly,
  Whether or near or far!

Whither it went, or what its quest,
  I know not; but one August day
A great white angel through the far
  Dim spaces took its way;

Until below it our fair earth,
  Like a rich jewel fitly hung —
An emerald set with silver gleams —
  In the blue ether swung.

The angel looked; the angel paused;
  Then down the starry pathway swept,
Till mount and valley, hill and plain,
  Beneath its vision slept.

Poised on a far blue mountain peak,
  It saw the land, from sea to sea,
Lifting in veilèd splendor up
  The banner of the free!

From tower and turret, spire and dome,
  From stately halls, and cabins rude,
Where crag and cliff and forest meet
  In awful solitude,

It saw strange, sombre pennants float,
  Black shadows on the summer breeze
That bore, from shore to shore, the wail
  Of solemn symphonies.

It saw long files of armèd men,
  Clad in a garb of faded blue,

23

Pass up and down the sorrowing land
　　As if in grand review,

It saw through crowded city streets,
　　Funereal trains move to and fro,
With tolling bells, and muffled drums,
　　And trumpets wailing low.

Descending then the angel sought
　　A stern, sad man of many cares;—
Ah, oft before have mortals talked
　　With angels, unawares!

The angel spake, as man to man:—
　　"What does it mean, O friend?" it cried,
"These sad-browed hosts, these weeds of woe,
　　This mourning far and wide?"

The stranger answered in amaze,—
　　"Know you not what the whole world knows?
To his long home, thus grandly borne,
　　Earth's greatest warrior goes.

" The foremost soldier of his age,
  The victor on full many a field —
Who saw the bravest of the brave
  To his stern prowess yield."

The angel sighed. " That means," it said,
  " Tumult and anguish, pain and death,
And countless sons of men borne down
  By the fierce cannon's breath ! "

Then passed from sight the heavenly guest,
  And from the mountain-top again
Took its far flight from North to South,
  Above the homes of men.

But still, where'er it went, it saw
  The starry banners half-mast high,
And tower and turret hung with black
  Against the reddening sky !

Still saw long ranks of armèd men
  Who for the blue had worn the gray —

Still saw the sad processions pass,
　　Darkening the summer day!

"Was this *their* conqueror whom you mourn?"
　　The angel said to one who kept
Lone watch where, deep in grass-grown graves,
　　Young Southern soldiers slept.

"Victor, yet friend," the answer came,
　　"Even theirs who here their life-blood poured!
He, when the bitter field was won,
　　Was first to sheathe the sword,

"And cry: 'O brothers, take my hand —
　　Brave foemen, let us be at peace!
O'er all the undivided land
　　Let clash of conflict cease!'"

The wondering angel went its way
　　From world to world, from star to star,
Where planet unto planet turned,
　　And suns blazed out afar.

" Learn, learn, O universe," it cried,
   " How great is he whose foemen lay
Their love and homage at his feet,
   On this — his burial day!"

THOU AND I.

APRIL days are over!
O my gay young lover,
Forth we fare together
In the soft May weather;
Forth we wander, hand in hand,
Seeking an enchanted land
Underneath a smiling sky,
    So blithely — thou and I!

Soft spring days are over!
O my ardent lover,
Many a hill together,
In the July weather,
Climb we when the days are long
And the summer heats are strong,
And the harvest wains go by,
    So bravely — thou and I!

July days are over!
O my faithful lover,
Side by side together
In the August weather,
When the swift, wild storms befall us,
And the fiery darts appall us,
Wait we till the clouds sweep by,
　　And stars shine — thou and I !

Summer days are over!
O my one true lover,
Sit we now alone together
In the early autumn weather!
From our nest the birds have flown
To fair dreamlands of their own,
And we see the days go by,
　　In silence — thou and I !

Storm and stress are over!
O my friend and lover,
Closer now we lean together
In the Indian-summer weather;

See the bright leaves falling, falling,
Hear the low winds calling, calling,
Glad to let the world go by
　　Unheeding — thou and I !

Winter days are over !
O my life-long lover,
Rest we now in peace together
Out of reach of changeful weather !
Not a sound can mar our sleeping —
Breath of laughter, or of weeping,
May not reach us where we lie
　　Uncaring — thou and I !